The big book Adventure

Written and illustrated by Rebecca Rose

The rain drip-dropped and the puddles plip-plopped.

And grey, grey, grey was the colour that day.

But scooting round puddles, without any troubles,

Two rainbow bright children whizzed on their way.

Twins, Zac and Sam, were out with their mam,

At a place where adventures begin.

A place of tears and laughter (and a happily ever after).

Of course! It's the library they're in.

Zac sat down and read, but Sam quickly said,
"I'm itching to go and explore."
And right at the back in the black, black, black
She found a book as big as a door.

A book so dusty, so smelly and musty,
It couldn't have been checked-out for ages.
She called to her brother, "Help me open this cover."
"I feel magic inside these pages."

Each grabbing a side, they opened it wide
And what they saw made them stop dead.
Because out from the page, stepped a young girl their age
With a hood of bright red, red, red.

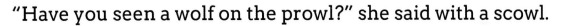

"Have you seen a wolf on the prowl?" she said with a scowl.

"I'm tracking one with the help of this book."

"I'm pursuing my passion for cutting-edge fashion;

And wolf-skin coats are the latest look."

Snaking slowly behind, a giant plant grew entwined.

(A veg' of prize-winning size!)

Each leaf, stalk and bean was green, green, green.

And from up high; they could hear Jack's cries.

"I'm here to look for a gardening book,

As my veg patch has really grown wild.

And fee fo fum, I'm in trouble with Mum.

Because our giant neighbour is really quite riled."

The twins were quite tickled by poor Jack's plant pickle,

They thought the young lad seemed canny.

Coming next. Why who? Shall I give you a clue?

What big teeth you have got Granny!

"Have you seen this child? She's really quite wild,"
The wolf eloquently asked of the twosome.
"Can I stick this on the wall, to warn one and all
That this child is vicious and gruesome?"

Twelve strikes from the clock and then... Wow! What a frock.

Her tiny glass shoe glitters blue, blue, blue.

"My goodness I'm late for an important date,"

Cinderella gasps whilst running through.

"I'm launching a line of glass slipper design,"
She calls back as she darts on her way.
"But the styles must be right and it's already midnight."
But Cinders, it's only midday!

She dashes on in a tizzy, the library is getting busy.

"We'll get into bother," Sam howls.

And then (even more scary), it's three bears
big and hairy,

And making the most terrible growls!

They're brown, brown, brown and all have a frown.

Someone ate their porridge you see!

But the growling and grumbling is just their tummies
rumbling.

They need a cookbook for a new recipe.

Sam's just shutting the cover, when out barges another
Much larger than life little girl.
She's cocky and bold, with hair of gold, gold, gold,
Each lock a perfect curl.

But looks can be deceiving, so don't go believing

This girl is all sweetness and honey.

She says, "Those bears had better beware.

I'm pic-NICKING their lunch for MY tummy."

"Phew," says Zac, "We've got to the back."
But that wasn't quite the end of the pages.
Wandering last, looking awfully downcast,
A princess who'd overslept by ages!

Her gown is rose, rose, rose; but so is her nose.

It is clear she has really been weeping.

"I'm in such a stew; this book is overdue."

"Will they be cross if I admit I was sleeping?"

And now the poor twins must try to fix things
As the library's all a hullabaloo.
There's noise and kerfuffle and even a scuffle
Over the bears' yummy chocolate fondue!

But just as the pair start to despair,

The Fairy Godmother saves the day.

Stepping from the book (with a teacher's stern look)

Her magic spell whisks the chaos away.

"Did anyone see?" says Sam,"Perhaps we should scram!"

And they slide the big book away with a swing.

But it seems they're in luck. Everyone's head is in a book.

And no-one has noticed a thing.

Really real big books

Rarely seen; barely read. Inside Newcastle City Library a collection of books sits on the shelf unseen.

Why? Because of their size. Too big to put on the shelves; not likely to fit in your book bag; and way too big to read on the bus or metro.

But in the summer of 2017 these big books were rediscovered by 22 of the region's artists, writers, performers, dancers and musicians.

Each artist created something unique and special inspired by this unusual collection of big books.

This children's book was inspired by my big book adventure. I hope you enjoyed it.

Rebecca

Find out more about our
Big Book Adventures
at
fsbaexhibition.wordpress.com